The Little Duck All the Luck

Written by
L.K. Brodie

Illustrated by
Kiran Akram

Illustrations: Kiran Akram
Book design: SWATT Books Ltd
Editing and proofreading: Craig Smith (CRS Editorial)

Printed in the United Kingdom.
First Printing 2024.

ISBN: 978-1-0687199-0-5

L. K. Brodie
Co. Cork, Ireland

This book belongs to

_____

Once, in a land so peaceful, lived a little duck who was ever so cheerful. He lived on the bank near a small pond, by some bushy trees that were ever so broad.

This little duck felt very different; because this little duck felt truly brilliant! He sometimes believed he might well be the luckiest little duck that ever lived.

One sunny morning, as mother duck sprang from the pond and shook herself dry, she called to the little duck and his three brothers and two sisters nearby.

"I have a big plan and I want you to hear it. Gather round little ducklings, gather round! Today is the day for your first big adventure! Today, you will swim in the big pond!"

They cheered rather loudly, with a lot of pleasure, and then formed a neat line behind their dear mother.

"Now, everyone please listen carefully to me! Stay close to me please and follow me quickly."

The little duck was at the front of the row, waddling away with a big smile on his face.

One of his sisters sadly behind him, jealously wondered how he got to the front and how she got the position unfairly behind him.

"How did you get that nice spot at the front by mother and I got this spot back here with the others?"

"I don't know the answer to the question you asked me, but it might well be because I am a lucky little duck!"

Along they waddled until, ever so sharply, mother duck
paused because they were at the end of their journey.

When the little duck got close to the big pond,
he moved to the side to see what he might see.

But his brothers and sisters were not paying much notice and
bumped up against their mother and fell flat on their faces!

"How come we fell, but you did not fall?"
said his jealous sister.

The little duck looked down to his sister and helped
her up from the ground, and then said to her,
sounding sure this time:
"I really must be a lucky little duck!"

The little duck and his brothers and sisters looked at the water, and watched their mother's actions and splashes with wonder, as she said: "Now, please watch me carefully. This is what you must do! Paddle with your feet and balance with them too. Your body will keep you floating, I can assure you of that, and in no time at all, you will be swimming like me."

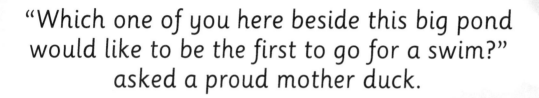

"Which one of you here beside this big pond would like to be the first to go for a swim?" asked a proud mother duck.

"Me, mother... me, mother... me, me, me! I want to be the first to go in swimming, please!"

Seeing the little duck and his brothers and sisters all hopping around with their wings in the air made it hard for the mother to choose who would be the first for a swim.

So, she closed her eyes tightly and pointed out with her wing, and when she opened her eyes widely she was pointing towards the little duck with all the luck!

"You can go first, but don't be too nervous, because I will be here, of that you can be certain," said mother duck.

"Oh, it does feel relaxing to be swimming around. Oh, it does feel so lovely to be here in this pond!" said the little duck.

When he came out of the water, his jealous sister went in after, but she could not pick up swimming as fast as her brother.

"I can't do it, mother. It is too hard and difficult! Why can't I swim as well as my brother?"

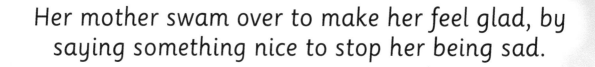

Her mother swam over to make her feel glad, by saying something nice to stop her being sad.

"It's OK you poor dear, just take your sweet time. Just calm yourself down and watch me again."

This made her feel good and then she got better, with each lap of the pond she did with her mother.

"That's how you do it! Now you are getting it! You are so brilliant! Keep up your fine effort!" said the little duck.

The little duck's brothers and other sister took their turn for a swim and got the hang of it after a while as well.

They all tried their hardest, but none of the other ducks could swim as fast as the little duck with all the luck.

"Gather round little ducklings, gather round! It is now time to go home. Before the night sets in, we must get home, before it gets dim," said mother duck.

The little duck with all the luck again led the group with his mother, with his jealous sister behind him, just like before.

"How come you swam quickly and made it look easy? And you got the front by mother again!" said his jealous sister.

"It must be because I am the luckiest little duck in the whole wide world!"

From that moment on, the little duck always succeeded. Everything he did, came very easy.

As he got older, much smarter and wiser, the little duck realised it was him who made his luck in life.

Once he learnt this, he found a neat trick! He learnt how to bring himself even more luck!

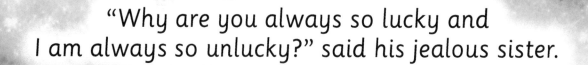

"Why are you always so lucky and
I am always so unlucky?" said his jealous sister.

"You too can be lucky, there is nothing that stops you.
But you must believe it is in you already!
You must believe luck is inside you, like me,
like I do, because that is the key to being so lucky!"

Sadly for the little duck's jealous sister, she never
believed him and continued to have the same bad luck.

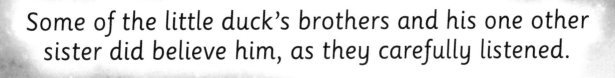

Some of the little duck's brothers and his one other sister did believe him, as they carefully listened.

And when they also realised they too had good luck, they then brought more luck their way!

Just like their lucky little brother...
the little duck with all the luck.

Milton Keynes UK
Ingram Content Group UK Ltd.
UKHW052023020824
446459UK00002B/13